# HOME FARM FRIENDS
## *Short Story Collection*

*Home Farm Twins*

# Home Farm Friends
*Short Story Collection*

Jenny Oldfield

Illustrated by Kate Aldous

*Hodder
Children's
Books*

a division of Hodder Headline

Typeset by Avon Dataset Ltd, Bidford-on-Avon, Warks

Printed and bound in Great Britain by
The Guernsey Press Co. Ltd, Channel Isles

Hodder Children's Books
a division of Hodder Headline
338 Euston Road
London NW1 3BH

# Contents

# *Speckle's lucky collar*

'Is this a great day out, or what?' Hannah Moore felt on top of the world as she rode her grey pony, Solo, high on the fell.

It was Spring Bank Holiday and Doveton village was crowded out with sightseers, but up here on wild Snakestone Pass, they were the only people around.

'It's OK for some!' Hannah's twin sister, Helen, grumbled. It was her turn to ride the bike. Ahead of her, Hannah and Solo, plus their friends, Laura Saunders on Sultan and Polly Moone on her drop-dead gorgeous chestnut horse, Holly, all

1

rode easily on to the high ridge.

'It's good exercise!' Laura turned to grin at the hot, struggling figure of Helen on her bike.

'Yeah, well you take this and I'll ride Sultan for you!' she retorted, glad that Speckle, the twins' faithful Border collie, had hung back to keep her company among the heather and bracken.

In any case, she didn't really mind. Hannah was right; this was a special day. The sky was blue, there was hardly any breeze, and the leather bags strapped to the horses' saddles contained sandwiches, crisps and big slabs of their mum's home-made chocolate fudge cake.

'Bad for you!' their dad had warned as the twins had saddled Solo back at Home Farm. 'Loadsa calories!'

'Don't care!' Helen and Hannah had sung back at him, patting their flat stomachs and eyeing their dad's spreading paunch. 'Chocolate; yum-yum!'

'Be back by tea-time!' he'd instructed. 'Stay together, and don't do anything I wouldn't do!'

'In that case, we'd better just stay in bed!' Hannah had joked.

'Hah-hah, very funny. But seriously, girls; take

care up at High Force. Remember there's a fast current that could sweep you clean over the edge of the waterfall. So strictly no swimming!'

His warning had gone in one ear and out of the other.

'Don't worry, Dad. We're not stupid!' they'd replied with an offhand wave.

And now all Helen could think about was working hard to keep up with the others. *Puff-puff-puff, pedal-pedal, bump*!

*Woof*! Speckle barked encouragement as Solo, Sultan and Holly carried their riders briskly beneath a canopy of old oak trees towards the fast-running stream that led to the secluded yet spectacular site of High Force waterfall.

'Fantastic, or what?' Hannah murmured as they reached the fall.

This was the first time that Polly had visited the place. The sound of rushing water, of leaves rustling and birds singing was almost too good to spoil with normal human chit-chat. It was like whispering in church.

'Magic.' Polly nodded and slipped from Holly's

back, holding tight to the chestnut's reins. She gazed up at the trees; down at the wide, clear stream tumbling over rocks towards the sheer edge of High Force.

'Don't let Holly go too near,' Laura reminded the younger girl, pointing twenty metres downstream. 'She could lose her footing and get swept into those rapids.'

'OK, I'll hold on to her reins while she takes a drink.' Rider and horse stepped gingerly towards the water's edge, aware of the rush and roar of the waterfall beyond a stretch of whirling white water.

'What about Solo?' Laura turned to Hannah.

Hannah didn't want to risk the stream. 'He's OK, he's not thirsty, thanks.'

'Yeah, neither is Sultan. Anyway, you know what he's like. He never gets his feet wet if he can possibly help it!'

Laura led her beautiful bay thoroughbred to the nearest stout branch and carefully tethered him. As Hannah dismounted and did the same, Helen finally rode up to join them.

'How come I get to ride this rotten thing up the

steepest bit?' she grumbled, throwing the bike to the ground as if it was the machine's fault that she was out of breath and aching. Then she sank on to the grass and flopped back, while Speckle came up and gave her a sympathetic nudge. 'No one cares except you, Speckle!' she muttered, catching hold of his worn leather collar and giving him a tired hug.

The dog settled beside her, resting his head on his grey speckled front legs, gently wagging his tail to and fro across Helen's body.

'. . . Tortilla chips, anyone?' Laura called as she perched on a rock by the stream. She'd opened her sandwich box and spread out its contents.

Tortilla chips! Helen sprang to her feet. Not just plain ordinary crisps . . . She sprinted across the small clearing to join her fair-haired friend.

'Thought you were exhausted!' Hannah said.

'Ignore her,' Polly advised Helen from the tree which she'd chosen to tether Holly to. 'Hey, it's too brilliant up here to argue. Anyway, Helen, when we set off again, I'll take the bike and you can ride Holly, OK?'

With a mouthful of tortillas, Helen's eyes lit up.

Holly was the envy of all the kids in Doveton: coat shiny and rich as a conker, a white flash down her beautiful face, white socks, long, flowing mane. The thought of riding the wonderful horse made Helen gobble her sandwiches and munch through her chocolate fudge cake in record time.

'What's with High Force?' Polly chatted while Helen ate. 'I mean, how come we're the only ones here?'

'It's miles from the nearest road,' Hannah pointed out. 'You get a few walkers doing the Three Peaks route. But not many people know this is a public right of way across the land belonging to Coningsby Hall.'

'So, it's like a secret?' Polly offered Speckle a chunk of cheese from one of her sandwiches. 'That makes it even more special, I guess.'

'There's a sad story about High Force,' Laura told her, then turned to Helen and Hannah. 'Do you know it?'

'The one about Lord Henry Coningsby?' Hannah nodded while Helen munched on.

'A hundred years ago, on a summer's evening, his young wife was riding back from Doveton . . .'

Laura emptied the bag of tortilla chips and packed it neatly back in her sandwich box, then continued. 'The mist came down as she rode through Snakestone Pass and her horse lost its way and stumbled into the stream in this very clearing!'

'Don't tell me!' Polly guessed the rest. 'They got caught in the current and dragged over the edge!'

'Lord Henry and his men found the bodies early next morning.' Standing up on their picnic rock, Hannah gazed the length of the rapids towards the sheer drop. 'The accident broke his heart. They'd only been married for three months and he was left alone, without any family. A week later, in the middle of a still, moonlit night, he came out here, stood by that tree on the flat rock by the waterfall . . .'

'. . . And jumped?' Polly whispered.

Laura and Hannah nodded silently.

'Tragic!' Polly sighed, listening to the roar of the water.

'Yeah; thanks Laura, thanks, Hannah!' Helen shook herself and scrambled down from their rock. 'That's just what we needed to know to make our day!' She shrugged apologetically at Polly.

'No, that's OK, it's dead romantic!' Polly sighed. Then she shook herself. 'I suppose it's time to move on.'

Over by the trees the tethered horses shifted their weight to reach for succulent leaves, while Speckle trotted nose to the ground around the picnic rock, eager to hoover up spilt crumbs.

But before they had time to pack their saddle-bags and put on their hard hats, there was a sudden disturbance on the bank opposite.

Speckle was the first to notice it. He raised his head and gave a sharp bark as a large, hairy, reddish-brown creature came lumbering between the trees.

'Aagh!' Polly squealed as the highland cow lurched down the bank, tossing her curved horns and bellowing back at the Border collie.

'It's OK, it's only one of Mr Cooke's kyloes,' Hannah reassured her. Terence Cooke was the gentleman farmer at Coningsby Hall, and she recognised the wild-looking cow as one of his. 'Look, here come a couple more.'

It was true; another full-sized cow and a half-grown calf followed their leader through the trees.

'But what are they doing out of their field? They're usually close to the Hall,' Helen said, realising that Eddie Huby, Terence Cooke's stockman, would never have let the cows near the dangerous waterfall. 'They must've escaped!'

The others agreed.

'What should we do?' Polly asked, working out that it would take ages to mount up and ride to the grand house to warn the cows' owner. She teetered on the bank of the stream, staring anxiously at the three clumsy creatures as they sank to their knees in mud on the far side.

'Hush, Speckle, good boy!' Helen tried to quieten the yapping dog. The Border collie was making short runs along the water's edge, darting at the cattle as if to turn them back.

But his bark only alarmed the youngest of the three cows. Instead of backing off from the fast-running water, the calf lurched forward, stumbled and went down on to her knees.

'Watch out!' Hannah cried, standing helpless as the water splashed and swirled up to the calf's shoulders.

The four girls froze, eyes fixed on the calf, not

noticing Speckle plunge into the stream until it was too late.

'No, come back!' Helen called to the bold Border collie. He'd seen the calf in danger and sprung into action, not realising how strong the current was in this part of the stream. There was a powerful undertow, unseen on the bright surface; a force that dragged at Speckle the moment he jumped in.

'Speckle!' Hannah saw their dog disappear under the water and then bob up a couple of metres downstream. On the far bank, the unwary calf had staggered to her feet and was pulling herself out of the mud, back up the bank. The two adult cows bellowed and trampled through the undergrowth, leading her to safety.

But the current had caught hold of the twins' precious dog and swirled him away. It dragged him under a second time, then sent him surging back to the surface only two or three metres from the crashing waterfall.

Speckle strained to keep his head above water, paddling furiously but unable to resist the current. Ten seconds and he would reach the edge . . .

seven, six, five seconds . . .

Hannah and Helen sprinted along the rocky bank, followed by Polly and Laura. They splashed ankle-deep into the water, stumbled over boulders, hearing the water crash, seeing Speckle glide closer to the edge.

Realising the danger, the dog made one last huge effort to swim to the bank. He made headway. Four seconds, three, two . . . A low branch hung out over the stream, its leaves dipping into the water. Speckle's head vanished into the leaves; the branch bent and dipped as if taking his weight.

Helen closed her eyes, unable to look.

'Where is he? What happened?' Laura gasped, catching up with Hannah.

'He's under that branch. I think his collar caught on a twig!' Hannah was only guessing that this was what had prevented the dog from sliding over the waterfall. She could see the edge and the five metre drop, broken by sharp boulders where spray bounced and splashed. And between the fluttering leaves she could spot Speckle's black head, and – yes, his old brown collar caught on a thin, spiky branch. It held his weight, but who knew for how long?

'Quick, Helen, we can save him if we all work together!' Hannah's thoughts raced. 'Polly, you work your way up the bank and grab hold of that tree trunk with one arm. Laura, you stand further down the bank and hold on to Polly's free hand. Helen, you make a longer chain, so that I can grab on to you and reach out into the water to rescue Speckle!'

Without pausing to think of their own safety, the three girls nodded and did as Hannah said. Soon they'd grasped each others' wrists and formed a human chain that allowed her to stand knee-deep in the stream and stretch out towards the struggling dog.

Hannah strained towards the low branch. Her fingertips were a few centimetres from Speckle's head. The current tugged at him, threatening to unhitch him from his twig and sweep him away. 'More!' Hannah gasped, feeling her arm almost pull out of its socket.

Polly, Laura and Helen stretched even further. A couple more centimetres and their wet fingers might slip and the chain snap.

Hannah strained again. Her fingers felt for Speckle's head, touched it, then slipped under the collar. She hooked two fingers, took his weight and dragged him towards her.

'Hold on!' Helen yelled. She saw Speckle's dripping body emerge from the stream. 'Hannah's doing it! She's pulling him clear!'

'It was a miracle that Speckle made it!' David Moore had been called to Coningsby Hall by Eddie Huby, along with Laura's mother and Polly's father. It was two hours after the dramatic rescue, which the stockman, arriving on the scene to fetch back his straying cattle, had witnessed from the far bank.

'I don't know about miracles.' Eddie shook his head. 'From what I saw when I arrived, it had more to do with Hannah's quick thinking.'

'Hannah was the hero!' Laura agreed. 'She saved Speckle's life!'

Soaked through, aching all over, trembling from the strain of it all, still Hannah managed a weak smile. She sat in the kitchen of Eddie's lodge, one arm around the Border collie, as if she still couldn't trust herself to let him go.

She relived the moment when her fingers had closed around the dog's collar, felt his weight as she dragged him out of the water, remembered how they'd laughed and cried over him when he finally stood on the bank, shook himself and showered them from head to foot.

This talk and attention made her blush, so she ducked her head and fingered the cold, smooth disc hanging from Speckle's neck. There was the name engraved in the metal, and she recalled how she and Helen had found the worn collar hanging from a door-hook at Home Farm on the day they'd moved into the old house.

They'd kept the collar and given it to their own dog in honour of the first Speckle: a champion sheepdog in his time and famous throughout the Lakes.

Smiling broadly now, she glanced up at Helen. 'Forget miracles and heroes,' she murmured. 'The reason Speckle lived was because he was wearing his lucky collar!'

## Stanley's close shave

'Helen Moore, what *do* you look like!' Sam Lawson crowed.

'I look better than you!' Helen retorted, uncomfortable under her tall wig of sticking-up yellow sponge. Her face, arms and legs were all yellow. Her T-shirt was pale blue and she wore dark blue shorts. She was dressed up as Bart Simpson for the Doveton Gala.

Sam's so-called fancy dress was the Man. United football strip.

'Dream on!' Hannah smirked as she strolled round the back of the red and white figure to read

**the name** of his favourite, fair-haired star player. 'Couldn't you think of anything more interesting than that?'

'You two look like you caught a deadly disease!' Sam wasn't put off. He crowed and jeered some more.

'We're the Simpsons!' Helen insisted. 'Hannah's Lisa and I'm Bart. So, "Eat my shorts!", Sam Lawson!'

The twins turned and walked away.

'Whose idea was this?' Helen muttered from under her layer of yellow face-paint. In spite of the brave front they'd put on for Sam's benefit, she was beginning to have doubts about the Bart Simpson brainwave.

'Dad's,' Hannah sighed, spying his shambling, untidy figure across the field.

David Moore was busy taking photographs of the village festival. There were flower stalls and morris dancers, a pet show and at least fifty other entrants for the fancy dress competition. And Gala Day meant that John Fox's lakeside field was decked out with long strings of coloured flags which fluttered in a light breeze blowing down from the steep, green side of Doveton Fell.

'Why couldn't we have nice, normal parents who dress us up in ordinary fancy dress?' Helen grumbled, loud enough for her mum to hear as they passed by the cake stall.

'Yeah, like footballers!' Hannah agreed. 'Or Red Riding Hood, or Pocohontas!'

Mary Moore laughed. 'You two look great!' she called after them. 'Very original. You're lucky you have such a creative father!'

'Foam-rubber wigs and yellow face-paint. Yeah!' Helen grumbled, walking on towards what was for them the major attraction: the local pets gathered for judging by Cecil Winter, the ex-head-teacher of the village school.

There were dogs and cats, a Shetland pony, rabbits, hamsters, a lamb and a cockatoo.

'Aah!' Helen cooed over a black, lop-eared rabbit called Sooty.

The rabbit shuffled to the front of his cage and peered out at the crowds. His droopy ears and hunched shape made him look fed up, until Helen bent down and put her yellow face up against the wire mesh. Then the rabbit bolted back into his sleeping compartment.

'You scared him!' Sam cawed, trailing 'Bart' and 'Lisa' wherever they went.

'Ohh!' Hannah pointed out a fluffy, pure white, long-haired cat snoozing in a cat-carrier in the afternoon sun.

The cat spotted her, stood up, arched her back and hissed.

'Ha-ha-ha-hah!' Sam laughed loudly.

'Ignore him!' Helen insisted, tripping over her giant, foam-rubber trainers as she walked on.

'Hey!' Hannah grabbed her arm and stopped them in their tracks. 'Do you see who I see?'

Further along the row of pets was a cage containing a small, golden-haired creature with beady black eyes and long white whiskers. There was a large white cardboard label propped against the cage, telling passers-by that this was the Satin-Coated Hamster Champion of the whole of the North of England.

Helen's eyes lit up. 'Stanley!' she gasped.

Stanley, the golden hamster! 'What's he doing here?' Hannah demanded, hurrying ahead of

Helen now to make sure that this really was him.

Yes; that was Stanley's little pink nose and dark brown ears. That was his chubby golden face, his soft, round shape . . . and this was his fearsome owner, Mrs Lucia Goodenough, bearing down on them!

'Shoo!' Mrs Goodenough cried. Dressed in bright pink, clutching her giant white handbag, her foghorn-voice scattered all before her. 'Stand back from Stanley!' she ordered the twins. 'Don't touch him. Stay back, whoever you are!'

'It's us; Hannah and Helen Moore,' Hannah tried to explain. 'You remember!'

She and Helen had once rescued Mrs Goodenough's prize hamster from the clutches of a slimy cheat called Cliff Walters.

'. . . Nasty, horrid children!' Lucia Goodenough swung out with her massive handbag at the two strange yellow creatures whom she'd caught interfering with her precious pet.

Helen and Hannah ducked.

'You frightened my poor little hamster!' *Whack*! The white handbag missed Hannah and smashed

21

into the table. *Bash! Thwack! Crunch*!

Then the chairperson of the Lakeland Hamster Club took Stanley's cage from the table where it sat and clutched it to her large bosom. 'Come to Mummy, Stanley, dear! She's not going to leave you sitting here a moment longer! No, you're coming with me to the nice refreshment tent!'

'B-but!' Hannah stammered.

'We didn't . . . do anything!' Helen's voice faded as Mrs Goodenough swept her prize hamster away.

'Ha-ha-ha-ha-ha-hah!' Sam's laughter followed the twins as they trailed off, away from the animals to the safety of the morris dancers and their jangling bells.

It turned out that Lucia Goodenough was visiting her old friend, Mr Winter.

Stanley had come too because the lady never went anywhere without him. Unlike her husband, George, who she often left behind to take care of the house and water the plants. But not Stanley. Wherever Lucia went, he went too.

'And she's been good enough to help me judge the pets competition,' the ex-headteacher told Hannah and Helen. 'Oh, I say; Mrs "Goodenough" has been "good enough" . . . ! Oh, aha, ha-ha!' He chuckled at his own little joke, his grey moustache twitching up and down on his top lip. Dressed as usual in his navy-blue blazer with bright silver buttons, the creases in his beige trousers were as well pressed as ever. 'Of course Stanley came along. Lucia didn't think it was fair to enter him into the contest, though; which I must say is extremely decent of her. The little chap would have swept away the opposition and come in an easy winner. As it is, she generously allowed a local person to take the prize!'

'Mrs Goodenough didn't even recognise us,' Helen complained.

The dancers had finished leaping and twirling their stout sticks and were making way for the main procession of the day. This was when a lorry decorated with flowers and ribbons would drive into the field bearing the Doveton Gala Queen and her attendants.

Mr Cecil sympathised with the twins. 'Yes, I

saw her go off with Stanley before you had a chance to get reacquainted.'

'But I think *he* knew who we were!' Hannah pointed out. 'Even though we're in fancy dress, his eyes seemed to kind of sparkle as if he remembered us!'

The old teacher looked down at her with a superior smile. 'I think you may be imagining things there, Helen, dear.'

'I'm Hann . . . !' She sighed and gave up.

'So, did you two little ducklings win a fancy-dress prize?' Mr Winter queried, waving to people in the crowd and beginning to clear a path, ready for the entrance of the Gala Queen.

'We're not ducklings, we're the Simp . . . Oh, never mind!' As the music announcing the arrival of the Queen's lorry began to blare over the loudspeakers, Helen too gave up.

'I don't want to watch this bit,' Hannah had told Helen crossly.

'Me neither.' Helen had led the way out of the crowd which crushed around the gate for a first view of the procession.

Polly Moone, the new girl at Manor Farm, was to be crowned queen for the year, taking over from Laura Saunders. Both girls would be sitting on the decorated lorry, wearing pastel-coloured, frilled dresses and little tiaras made out of artificial flowers.

'Why don't you two girls enter the Gala Queen competition?' their dad had asked, way back in early spring.

'Yuck!' Helen and Hannah had replied as one.

'Let's go . . .' Hannah had begun.

'And take a peep . . .' Helen's eyes had lit up.

'. . . at Stanley instead!' Hannah had finished off.

Which is why they were heading back to the refreshment tent while everyone else was making their way to see the procession.

'You're going the wrong way!' Sam called, when he spotted them crossing the field. 'What's up? Got a bad case of "yellow" fever, ha-ha!'

Helen grimaced and fumed. 'I'll . . . I'll . . . !'

'Never mind him. There's Stanley!' Hannah pointed to a table outside the big refreshment tent where Lucia Goodenough was carefully placing the hamster's cage. The large, bright pink lady

25

with the loud voice was talking to her little, long-haired champion as if he understood every word.

'Now, dear; if Mummy puts you inside your nice clear plastic cleaning-ball while she cleans out your cage, you'll have a wonderful view of all the exciting things that are going on!' Carefully Mrs Goodenough opened Stanley's cage door and lifted him out. She cradled him in both hands, holding his fat little body up to her face and giving him a playful cuddle. '*Mwah, mwah, mwah*!'

Stanley squeaked and squirmed.

'Now, don't nip Mummy's finger with those sharp little front teeth!' Lucia told him, hastily putting an end to the cuddles and popping the hamster inside a plastic ball the size of a football, which she then placed on the grass beside the table.

'Aah!' Hannah whispered, careful to stay back behind a nearby stall. She could just see Stanley scrabble around inside the clear ball, his little feet rocking it to and fro.

'Careful Mrs G doesn't see us!' Helen warned, eager to avoid being shooed off again. But she too was dying for a closer look.

And it seemed their luck was in. Because, just then Mr Winter came marching up.

'Lucia!' he called. 'You're needed in the Communications Tent, A S A P! We'd like you to announce the arrival of the Gala Queen. Come quickly!'

'But – oh, very well!' Mrs Goodenough, flattered by the request, was prepared to drop everything and go with Mr Winter. 'Give me a moment while I pop Stanley back into his cage.'

'No time! The lorry is about to turn into the field.' Mr Winter flapped his hand in the direction of the gate, grabbed the guest of honour and led her quickly away . . .

Leaving Stanley alone on the grass!

'C'mon!' Hannah seized her chance. She sprinted across to the refreshment tent as fast as her costume allowed.

Helen fumbled and tumbled after her in her cartoon trainers.

They dropped to their knees beside the hamster's cleaning-ball and peered inside.

Stanley stared out, whiskers twitching, a look of alarm on his fat little golden face.

'It's us!' Hannah insisted. She poked her yellow face right up to the ball. 'Remember – Cliff Walters – you ran away – chocolate cake!'

But Stanley wasn't listening. '*Let me out of here*!' he thought, scrabbling with his sharp claws at the smooth plastic surface. '*Help! Aliens! Monsters from outer space*!'

As he scrabbled, the ball rocked. It rocked harder and shifted, making Stanley run inside the ball like a pet mouse inside a treadmill.

'Watch it!' Helen warned as the ball moved a few centimetres across the grass.

At the far side of the field, Mrs Goodenough took the microphone and made her announcement. 'Ladies and gentlemen, it is with great pleasure, on behalf of the Doveton Gala Committee, that I present this year's Queen, Miss Polly Moone!'

A lorry decked out with flowers and ribbons slowly entered the arena and began a slow circuit. The crowd clapped and cheered at both Polly and Laura, and their four little attendants.

Inside his plastic ball, Stanley began to trundle in earnest. *Plod-plod-plod* inside the plastic shell, gathering speed as the twins stood by.

'Grab him!' Hannah cried, suddenly alarmed.

A hamster inside a cleaning-ball could easily get crushed by the crowd making its way across the field as the decorated lorry made its tour.

'Too late!' Helen made a desperate rugby-tackle just at the moment when Stanley reached a downwards slope. The ball picked up more speed; *bump-bump* over the rough grass, with Stanley's short legs working overtime to keep up.

One dizzy hamster, two surprised girls.

'Oh no!' Helen gasped.

Stanley was trucking on, rolling down the slope and out into the path of the crowd.

'Stop that hamster!' Hannah cried.

'Hey, look at Lisa Simpson throwing a wobbler!' Sam Lawson jeered from amongst the cheering crowd.

'Sam, we're serious! Stop that ball!' Helen sprinted down the slope as fast as her shoes would allow.

Too late again. Sam, in his Man. United strip, had missed his chance to be a hero. Their worst fear of all was actually happening; Stanley and the ball were rolling down the hill, through the crowd towards the approaching lorry!

'He'll be crushed!' Hannah gasped.

The lorry drove slowly and sedately on. Stanley rolled dizzily towards the giant black tyres. *Bump-bump, bounce-bump*!

'Not if I can help it!' Helen cried.

She sprinted; an awkward figure in a spiky yellow wig, down the slope, through the crowd, after the runaway hamster.

'He'll be squashed, squidged, splattered!' Hannah moaned. The driver of the lorry drove on regardless.

But Helen gained on Stanley. She braved the warning yells of the crowd and the looming shape of the Gala Queen's wagon. She reached the rolling ball, stooped, scooped it up with both hands and ran like a rugby player scoring a try, clear of the lorry.

'. . . My heroine!' Mrs Goodenough said of Helen, once she got over what had happened. 'So careless of Mummy to leave poor little Stanley unattended inside his silly plastic ball! She promises never to do it ever again!'

Helen stood with Stanley cradled in her hands, stroking his soft golden fur. She could feel his little heart pounding fast from his wild run inside the ball.

In the middle of the field, the crowd clapped as Laura Saunders handed over the Gala Queen crown.

'Good job the lorry was going so slowly!' Mary Moore had only just managed to open her eyes and check that both Stanley and Helen were safe. 'Helen, promise me you'll never ever do anything like that again!' she begged her brave but reckless daughter.

'Here, let me have a hold,' Hannah asked, smiling as she took Stanley from Helen. The hamster's whiskers tickled her fingers, his feet scrabbled on the palm of her hand. 'Guess what I've got for you!'

Chocolate cake! A big chunk of it from the refreshment tent. Stanley's favourite.

The hamster blinked up at Hannah. *Squeak, squeak*! He took a giant chunk and held it between his front paws, nibbling with his sharp front teeth and storing crumbs greedily in his wide cheek pouches.

Hannah grinned at Helen, who smiled proudly back.

*Chomp-chomp-chomp*. Hamster heaven!

# *A portrait of Scott*

' *"This is how the lady rides; nim-nim-nim*!

*This is how the gentleman rides; trot-trot-trot*!" '

Laura Saunders sang the old nursery rhyme for Joe Stott as she led Scott the Shetland pony round the paddock at Doveton Manor.

Leaning on the white fence, Helen and Hannah stood and watched.

'Joe looks tiny in that saddle,' Hannah murmured.

'But Scott is taking good care of him.' Helen knew that the good-natured pony was as safe as could be.

Hannah agreed. 'Listen to Joe. He's trying to say the rhyme too!'

' "*Dis . . . farmer . . . gallopy-gallop!*" ' The tiny, fair-haired boy joggled up and down in the saddle as Scott walked steadily on.

' "*And this is how the old man rides; cloppety . . . cloppety!*' Smiling, Laura released the lead rope and stretched out both arms to catch the toddler as he giggled and tipped sideways towards her. ' "*Cloppety . . . into the ditch!*" '

Joe squealed and she caught him, swung him round and handed him safely back to his mum, who stood nearby.

'Aah, sweet!' Hannah sighed.

Julie Stott had let Joe squirm around in her arms to stroke Scott. His plump fingers caught in the pony's shaggy mane and Laura had to untangle them. But Scott stood patiently, ears pricked towards the little boy, waiting until his hand was free.

'Scott's so gentle!' Helen too felt her heart melt. The sturdy pony had been through hard times; the twins and Laura had found him tethered and half-starved on a Scottish hillside along with

Heather, a piebald foal. But the bad treatment hadn't soured his temper, and now that Laura had adopted both Scott and Heather, he made the ideal ride for a tiny boy like Joe.

' "*Dis . . . farmer . . . gallopy*!" ' Joe cried again, wriggling and pleading to be let back on to the pony.

But Julie Stott said no, it was time to go home to Clover Farm. She thanked Laura for letting Joe ride the pony, while Helen climbed the fence and ran to offer to unsaddle Scott.

'Any time,' Laura smiled back at Julie and squeezed Joe's hand. 'You're welcome to bring him again.'

'Maybe after . . . tomorrow,' Julie stammered. Her smile faded, though Helen guessed she was trying to keep up a brave front. It seemed there was something the young mother didn't want to talk about in front of her son.

'Yeah, sure!' Laura cut in quickly. 'I understand. And good luck, OK?'

'Thanks.' Backing away with Joe, Julie nodded. She left quietly, heading for the Land Rover parked in the Saunderses' stable yard.

'Why does Julie need good luck?' Hannah asked, approaching the group as Helen unbuckled Scott's girth strap to slide the saddle from his broad back. In some strange way, the happy atmosphere of the afternoon ride seemed to have evaporated.

Laura sighed and gazed after the retreating figures of the mother and son. 'Haven't you heard? The Stotts have to take Joe into hospital for major surgery.'

The news made Hannah gasp. 'Why? What's wrong with him? Is it serious?'

Stroking Scott's hairy cheek, Laura nodded. 'They say there's a problem with his heart. Having this operation is his only chance,' she told them quietly. 'Apparently tomorrow's the big day.'

'Poor Julie and Dan!' The phrase was on everyone's lips. The whole of Doveton found it all too easy to imagine how worried the parents must be.

'. . . So young to have such a big operation!' Mary Moore sighed when the twins told her the news. 'Those doctors have to be very clever to deal with such a small boy!'

'. . . Doesn't bear thinking about,' David Moore murmured, quietly arranging newly-printed photographs of a badger into neat piles on the kitchen table.

Hannah and Helen couldn't believe it was happening.

'Joe looked so . . . normal!' Hannah breathed. 'He was riding Scott as if there was nothing wrong!'

'But his mum looked worried,' Helen recalled. 'And Laura's sure the operation is happening. Her dad knows the surgeon in Manchester who's going to do it.'

'So we keep our fingers crossed,' Mary said, staring sadly out of the window at the setting sun. 'And let's hope it all goes well.'

'. . . How's Joe Stott?' Carrie Lawson asked when she arrived to collect Sam from school. It was the question on everyone's lips.

Miss Wesley, Hannah and Helen's teacher, shook her head. 'No news yet.'

'. . . Have you heard how the operation went for the Stotts' little lad?' Fred Hunt asked John Fox as the two old farmers met up outside Luke Martin's shop.

'No, nothing.' John shrugged. He'd just checked with Luke, who thought that they wouldn't get any news that day. 'Luke says Dan and Julie plan to stay overnight at the hospital. He's arranged to shut up shop early and pop over to their place to keep an eye on things until they get back.'

Hannah and Helen took in these details without saying a word. There were dozens of questions they could have asked, but no one would know the answers. They just had to wait.

'Joe's in intensive care.' The twins' dad came off the phone early next morning. 'That was Luke. He's heard that there were complications during the operation. The doctors say it's touch and go.'

'Poor little thing!' As usual, Mary was in a rush to leave for work, but the news made her sit heavily at the table and ask for another cup of tea.

'So what happens now?' Hannah asked. Intensive care . . . complications. It didn't sound good.

Mary sipped her tea. 'More waiting.'

'Try not to worry,' the twins' dad advised. 'Joe is being well looked after. The nurses and doctors know exactly what they're doing. We just have to trust them.'

'Oh, but poor Dan and Julie!' Despite David's reassurance, Mary let her feelings show. 'I only wish there was something we could do!'

'I want to help!' Helen told Hannah.

Two days had gone by, and still the whole village held their breath over Joe Stott. Word from the hospital came via Luke, who told people that though there was no obvious reason why the toddler should not recover from the surgery, still the doctors were at a loss to explain why he was so slow to make progress.

'It seems he's conscious and out of intensive care, but not taking any interest in things around him,' Luke told David and the twins. They'd called in at the shop after school, especially to ask after the little patient. 'Dan says they can't get him to eat, and he hasn't said a single word to anyone since he came round.'

His comment had made Helen feel the same as

her mum two days before: helpless, yet at the same time longing to think of something positive they could do.

'The hospital says no visitors,' Luke reported. 'Of course, Joe's mum and dad are still at his bedside.'

'Why don't we send a card?' Hannah sifted through the rack of flowery greetings cards on Luke's counter. 'This is cute!' She picked up one with a picture of fluffy yellow chicks on the front and a 'Get Well Soon' message inside.

Helen considered the card. 'The only problem is, Joe's too young to read it.'

Hannah sighed and went on looking. 'Yeah, and we don't know if he likes chickens that much . . .'

'He *does* like horses,' Helen murmured, picking out a card with a picture of a chestnut thoroughbred.

'Hey, yeah! Is there one of a Shetland pony?' Hannah asked Luke.

'Sorry, that's all there is.' The shopkeeper had moved on to serve another customer.

'A Shetland pony would be good,' Hannah muttered stubbornly. 'Especially one that looks like Scott. Don't you think that would cheer Joe up loads, Helen?'

As Hannah went on searching, Helen's dark brown eyes narrowed. She focused on the camera her dad was carrying after his day's work photographing John Fox's prize Herdwick sheep. 'Hannah, you're a genius!' she whispered.

'I am?' Still Hannah couldn't find exactly the card she wanted. One with a cute picture of a small black and white Shetland pony; the sort that Joe would be bound to recognise.

'Yeah, you're brilliant!' Moving quickly, Helen seized David's camera. 'Dad, you don't mind if we borrow this, do you?'

'What? No, I suppose not, as long as you look after it!' he yelled, as Helen grabbed Hannah by the arm and dragged her out of the shop. 'Where are you off to now?'

'Now, Scott, you have to stand still and look straight into the camera!' Helen told the little pony.

Hannah had brushed Scott from head to toe. His black mane flowed down his neck and over his forehead, his long tail swished like silk. 'I get it!' she'd said, after Helen had rushed her down to Doveton Manor. 'We ask Laura if we can take a portrait of Scott, so we can make our own get-well card!'

'. . . Excellent!' Laura had agreed with the plan. 'Joe loved riding him. If he gets a card with the pony's picture on the front, it could be just what he needs to put him on the road to recovery!'

'We hope!' Hannah had whispered, eagerly grooming a patient Scott. A lot depended on this portrait. 'Make it a good photo!' she told Helen.

So Helen got close up and pointed the camera, Through the viewfinder she could make out the black mane and face with the bright white star on the forehead. Scott was looking back at her, bright and alert, head up, ears pricked, almost as if he knew that he had to put on his best front. 'Great!' she murmured. 'Now, hold it like that!'

*Click-whir. Click-whir. Click.* She took three quick shots.

Scott blew gently through his wide nostrils and curled his lip to show his big front teeth.

'He looks as if he's smiling!' Hannah cried. 'Take some more!'

*Click*. 'Perfect!' Helen took several rapid shots until she was sure she'd got enough. 'Now all we have to do is take them home and get Dad to help us develop them!'

'What d'you think?' Helen and Hannah had trimmed and glued the best portrait of the pony to a piece of bright yellow card. Now Hannah showed the result to their mum.

Mary nodded her approval. 'Very sweet!'

'Scott's smiling!' Happy with the result, Helen began to print the message inside the card.

David looked over her shoulder as she worked at the kitchen table. 'Can horses smile?' he wondered.

'Scott can!' Hannah insisted. She signed her name, impatient to set out on the hospital visit. This was Saturday, four days after Joe's operation, and their dad had agreed to drive them all the way to Manchester especially to hand-deliver the card. There was a knot in her stomach as she went through the day ahead: calling at the manor to collect Laura, making the two hour drive, finding the ward Joe was in . . .

Everything seemed to take forever. There was too much traffic on the motorway, a long queue to take them into the hospital car park. Hannah, Helen and Laura sat tensely in the car as David Moore paid the fee and found a space.

Then the hospital building was big and confusing. The corridors were long and spotlessly clean. Trolleys squeaked, people in white coats walked silently by.

'Yuck to the smell!' Hannah whispered. A hygienic hospital smell that you didn't get anywhere else.

Small wards led off from the corridors. Children sat on white beds surrounded by toys and books. The twins' dad asked at a desk which bed belonged to Joe Stott. A nurse told them, then asked if they were members of Joe's family.

'It's OK, they're good friends.' Dan Stott had spotted the visitors and interrupted the nurse at the desk. He smiled wearily at David and the girls. 'It's good of you to come all this way.'

'How's Joe?' Laura asked.

'More or less the same,' Dan admitted. His broad, normally smiling face was lined with worry. 'He still hasn't said a word since he came round. Poor little chap, I don't think he realises what's happening.'

Producing the special card from behind her back, Helen took a deep breath. 'We thought he might like this,' she said quietly, shy now that the moment had come.

Dan Stott looked at the portrait of Scott and nodded. 'That's a lovely idea,' he said, without much hope in his voice. 'Would you like to give it to him yourselves?'

So he led them to his son's bedside, where Julie sat trying to get Joe to eat some scrambled egg. Hannah saw how little and lost he looked in the hospital bed, how his fair curls were flattened, his eyes dull and listless.

'Hello, Joe!' Helen said softly, holding the card out for him to take.

The toddler turned to his mum to hook his arms around her neck and hide his head.

'It breaks your heart,' Dan muttered. 'This isn't like Joe at all. He used to be such a happy little soul!'

'Joe, we brought you a nice picture,' Laura said

gently. 'Don't you want to look?'

'It's a horse,' Hannah told him. 'Nice horse. You like this horse!'

Slowly Joe turned so they could see his eyes. He gazed blankly at the card which Helen had put face down on the bed.

'Would you like to see the picture?' she asked the still silent little boy.

Joe moved his head; the ghost of a nod.

Hannah turned the card face up. 'Here it is.'

And Scott the Shetland pony was looking up at Joe, ears pricked, lips curled back, looking for all the world as if he was smiling.

*Please let this work*! Helen prayed. *Let it be the thing that makes Joe want to get better*!

'Who's that?' Julie coaxed, picking up the portrait of Scott so that Joe could see it better. 'It's Scott, isn't it? You remember, Joe. This is Laura's pony; *"nim-nim-nim"*!'

A light came into Joe's blue eyes. He glanced from Laura to Helen and Hannah, and then back at the card.

*It's working*! Hannah thought. She held her breath, watching the little boy's every movement.

Joe pointed his finger at the picture of Scott. And, for the first time since the operation, a smile spread over his round, freckled face. At last, he spoke. '*Dis ... farmer ... gallopy-gallop*!' he gurgled. '*Cloppety-clop*!'

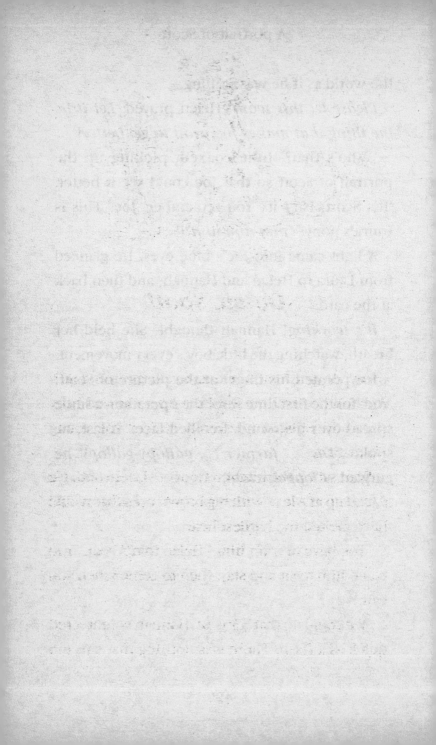

## Down, Spot!

'How do you teach a dog to do as he's told?' Alexa Wood wailed. She held up a chewed baby shoe and wagged it severely at Spot the young Dalmatian.

Spot sat on the kitchen floor at Hazelwood. He gazed up at Alexa with big brown eyes that would have melted the hardest heart.

'You have to train him,' Helen told Alexa. 'You teach him to sit and stay, then to come when you call.'

'*We* could do that for you!' Hannah volunteered quick as a flash. There was nothing that she and

Helen would like better than to work with the lively spotty dog.

'Hannah's the expert!' Helen said proudly. 'Watch!'

So Hannah took the chewed shoe from the harrassed young mother. 'Bad dog!' she said in a stern voice, waving it at Spot.

The dog's head went down, his ears drooped.

'Food – yes! Shoes – no!' Hannah insisted, putting the sorry sight on the table in between Alexa's toddler son, Daniel, and baby Ellie in her special canvas seat. The baby was giggling and wiggling her bare toes as Hannah gave Spot his first training session.

'Now, sit!' Hannah commanded. 'Stay!'

Spot knew he was in disgrace. He sat quietly on the kitchen tiles.

'Good dog!' Hannah said brightly.

Wagging his thin tail, Spot cocked up his ears.

'Good. Now, come here!'

Her pleased voice told him he was off the hook. He sprang forward. With one leap he was at Hannah's side, jumping up and licking her face.

'No, Spot!' Hannah wrestled with the

bundle of energy. 'Stay down, there's a good boy!'

'He doesn't understand the word "down" yet,' Helen explained hastily to an amused Alexa.

'That must be lesson 2!' She laughed. 'Anyway, enough training for one day. How about hot chocolate and toasted teacakes?'

It was just the sort of day for this kind of treat: cold and wet, with a blustery wind blowing from the lake. Hazelwood was a big house on the hill, tall and lonely, surrounded by trees. And Helen and Hannah were spending the day there to help Alexa look after the two children while her husband, Simon, and her mother-in-law, Marilyn Higham, travelled north to an art exhibition in Glasgow.

Mrs Higham was a famous artist who had paintings on view in the exhibition. She did her work in the studio across the yard from the house, and was often to be seen in Doveton village, her grey hair piled untidily on top of her head, her white shirt spattered with multi-coloured paint. Absent-minded and a bit aloof, it was only since she'd owned the Dalmatian that the twins had felt they might like to get to know the old lady from the big house on the hill. In fact, offering to help babysit the Wood children had really been Helen-and-Hannah-speak for looking after adorable Spot.

'It's a pity about the weather,' Alexa Wood remarked as she handed Hannah and Helen their teacakes and cut up one especially for Daniel and baby Ellie. Soon Ellie had smeared melted butter all over her face. 'If it had been fine, you could have taken Spot for a walk.'

'We could take him anyway!' Helen suggested. A drop of rain and the deepening evening gloom didn't put her and Hannah off.

Alexa glanced out at the downpour. Rain drove against the window and wind bent the branches of the trees. 'It's already getting dark, so maybe another time.'

From his high-chair, Daniel banged his plastic plate on the tray and pointed wildly across the table.

'What? – Oh, Spot!' his mum cried. She spied the Dalmatian mid-jump as he sprang up to steal a piece of teacake. 'Bad boy! Stay down!'

Too late. Spot sneaked a delicious toasted morsel

from the pile and gobbled it down.

Hannah frowned and strode towards him. 'Spot, that is not allowed!' She stood hands on hips staring sternly down.

The dog looked up and licked his lips.

'That is very, very bad!' Hannah insisted.

Spot's head drooped, he gazed up with pleading eyes. *Please don't be cross with me*!

'Perhaps you could take him for a short walk after all.' A weary Alexa changed her mind. 'He could run off some of that excess energy.'

'Great!' This was what Helen had wanted all along: a chance to dash down to the lakeside with Spot, to throw sticks for him to fetch, to watch his lithe, spotted shape race along the shore. She fetched her and Hannah's jackets and quickly got ready to brave the elements.

'Just a short walk, mind!' Alexa stood at the open door, watching them zip up their jackets. 'Don't wander too far, and make sure you're back before dark!'

'How c-cold are you?' Hannah gasped.

'Not c-cold at all!' Helen lied.

They'd taken Spot down to the pebble beach and walked him along the water's edge, as planned. Spray from the lake had blown into their faces, rain had battered them from every direction. The young dog had run and jumped, caught sticks, rolled, tumbled and raced madly after ducks, who had fled quacking from the spotted whirlwind.

'How w-wet are you?' Hannah flicked droplets of rain from her nose and shook her sodden fringe.

Helen stood at the gate to Hazelwood and peered out from under her hood. *Splash*! A giant, icy-cold drop landed on her cheek. *Splish-splash-splat*! The tree above showered her anew. 'S-soaked!' she admitted through chattering teeth.

'C'mon, let's get inside quick as we can!' Hannah led the way up the steep drive, feeling the wind buffet her. 'Which way did Spot go, did you see?'

'No, *you* let him off the lead. Didn't you watch where he went?' Helen wasn't worried. The last she'd seen of the young Dalmatian, he was sneaking through a gap in the fence and charging up the sloping lawn towards the house.

Hannah stopped and scanned the empty garden. The beech trees creaked in the wind, which tore ragged autumn leaves from their branches. And still the rain drove hard against the tall, gabled house, into the overflowing gutters and flooded drains. 'I guess he went around the back.'

'Let's hope so.' Even Helen didn't feel up to any more fun and games from Spot. She marched purposefully across the yard, ignoring the strange gurglings in the drain outside Mrs Higham's studio and the loose shutter banging against a nearby wall. 'Spot!' she called. 'Here, boy!'

The rain bounced from the stone-flagged yard. Hannah jumped a wide puddle and was heading for the back door of the house when Spot flew madly out of the alleyway between the studio and the bolted, windowless storeroom beside it.

'Down!' she yelled, as the Dalmatian leaped up against her, almost knocking her back into the puddle.

Spot veered away and jumped up against Helen.

'Spot, I'm already soaked to the skin!' Helen moaned. 'This isn't a good time for playing games.'

He yapped and jumped, twisted in mid-air, charged back towards Hannah.

The loose shutter banged again, and the window flew open, almost wrenched off its hinges by the wind. The noise drove Spot crazier than ever, making him charge at the open window, then dash back down the alley from which he'd emerged.

'We'll never get him inside the house at this rate,' Hannah grumbled, stomping off through the puddles to fetch him.

The alley was dark; a dead end which led only to a narrow side door into Mrs Higham's studio.

'Why isn't this window shut?' Helen wondered, deciding to try to close it while Hannah looked for Spot. It seemed likely that the absent-minded artist had left it off the latch for the wind to fling open.

*Yap-yap-yap*! Spot's high bark grew fainter as he fled down the alley.

'That's funny!' Taking hold of the window and pushing it to, Helen noticed there were raw marks in the frame, as if someone had forced it open. The wood was split and splintered and the iron clasp hanging loose. 'Hannah!' she called, her voice rising.

There was no answer. And strangely, Spot had stopped barking. What was going on? Helen gulped and raised herself on tiptoe to peer through the window.

The inside of the studio was gloomy, but she could make out large canvases propped against a wall, and shelves stacked with paint, glass jars and brushes. There was an easel in one corner, some empty picture frames in another. 'Hannah?' Helen hissed into the empty room. 'Where are you?'

'Here!' a voice said from behind her back.

Helen jumped and staggered back.

'Sorry.' Hannah shrugged: 'Spot took me on a wild goose chase down the alley. I tried the side door but it was locked, so I came back.'

'Where is he now?' Helen's teeth were still chattering, but now she wasn't sure if it was only from the cold. That was one spooky studio, with all its shadowy nooks and crannies. Then there were the bones, fossils and other natural objects that Mrs Higham had collected on a trestle table in the middle of the room.

'Good question.' Hannah turned to look round the yard, in time to see the eager dog gather himself for a charge straight at the window where they stood. 'No, Spot!' she warned. 'Down! Don't even think about it!'

'. . . Duck!' Helen cried as Spot ignored Hannah.

The girls crouched down while the Dalmatian leaped. He landed on the windowsill, got his balance, barked, then jumped down into the dark room.

'Huh!' Helen was the first to stand up. This was more than messing about; this was downright craziness. One silly young dog; one high, narrow window . . .

'Maybe he's looking for Mrs Higham?' Hannah suggested, clear-thinking as ever. 'Or maybe for some reason we don't know about, he's trying to get us to follow him in there!'

'No way!' Helen began. Then she remembered the broken catch. Broken catch – paintings in an empty studio – clever Spot trying to warn them. 'Hannah, how much is a painting by Marilyn Higham worth?' she whispered, clutching her sister's arm and dragging her away from the window.

'What?' I don't know! Thousands of pounds probably.' For a while, Hannah thought Helen had flipped. 'What kind of qustion is that?' she demanded, pulling herself free.

Still crouching, Helen pointed to the loose catch and splintered wood. 'Burglars!' she mouthed. 'In the studio! That's what Spot was trying to tell us, only we were too stupid to work it out!'

'You're crazy!' It was Hannah's turn to shake her head in disbelief.

'OK, then. Why is this catch broken? Why is Spot so keen to get us to follow him in?' By this time Helen was convinced.

'There could be hundreds of other reasons! The wind could've broken the catch. Spot could be messing about as usual!' To prove her own theory, Hannah got ready to climb in through the window. She heaved herself on to the sill, peering into the gloom.

'No, Hannah, wait!'

'You stay here, I'll unlock the side door from the inside and bring Spot out.' Without hesitating,

Hannah jumped into the studio.

Helen waited for what seemed like an age. Then she too hauled herself level with the sill. 'Hann?'

'Yep, I'm here, and so's Spot. No nasty thieves stealing paintings. It's quite safe!'

Making out Spot's black and white figure nosing under shelves and the damp, hooded shape of Hannah trying in vain to unbolt the side door, Helen judged that it was safe to follow. A few seconds later, she too was inside the artist's workshop.

'This bolt's stuck!' Hannah complained.

'Mind out, Spot!' Helen almost tripped over him as she went to help. She didn't like the smell of paint, or the way the wind caught the curtain across an alcove and made it billow towards her in a ghostly way. As she passed the table, she accidentally knocked a sheep's skull to the floor, where it broke into small pieces. 'Ugh!' She shuddered and moved on.

Still managing to get under Helen's feet, Spot jumped sideways as the skull fell. He sped off across the room towards the billowing curtain, sniffing hard at the hem and whining loudly.

'Help me pull the bolt,' Hannah told Helen. The studio was beginning to give her the creeps too. Burglars or no burglars, the sooner they got out of here the better.

Spot whined and pawed at the heavy grey curtain. He grabbed it between his teeth and pulled hard.

'Stop that, Spot!' Helen told him, glancing over her shoulder as she and Hannah continued to tug at the bolt.

He growled and ducked under the curtain so that only his back end showed. Then he gave a full-blooded bark.

'Ouch!'

Helen and Hannah froze at the sound of a man's voice crying out. They held their breaths.

Shapes behind the curtain struggled. The curtain tore and fell. Behind it was Spot and a cowering figure.

'I said, "Ouch!" ' the man cried. 'Get this dog off me, someone!'

'So, it *was* a burglar stealing Mrs Higham's paintings after all!' Helen crowed to Hannah.

The police had hurried up from Doveton in answer to Alexa Wood's emergency call. Spot had kept the thief at bay long enough for them to make an arrest and take the man off to the station.

'Not a very *good* burglar,' Hannah pointed out, remembering how the curtain had ripped as Spot had tugged at it, revealing a skinny man in his twenties with short, dark hair, wearing a black jacket with white stripes down the sleeves. 'And, luckily for us, he was a burglar who happened to be scared of dogs!'

'Not a good qualification for the job!' Alexa managed to laugh now that the excitement was over. She stood resting Ellie on one hip and holding on to Daniel with her other hand. 'A burglar with a phobia about dogs is like a sailor who's scared of the sea!'

Spot had growled and snapped, sunk his teeth into the man's trouser leg and generally terrified him until the police had arrived.

'But what I'm trying to say is that Spot was right all along!' Still breathless, Helen pointed out that if it hadn't been for the young Dalmatian, the thief would probably have escaped with a valuable canvas.

Hannah nodded. 'Yes, and we thought he was just fooling around as usual!'

'*You* thought!' Helen corrected her.

'OK, *I* thought,' Hannah admitted. She went over to where Spot sat, head to one side, a look of bright expectation on his sweet, spotted face. 'So, I should have trusted you, shouldn't I?'

Spot tipped his head to the other side, ears cocked, lapping up the praise. He seemed to know he'd been the hero of the hour.

'Yes, you should!' Helen agreed. Then she looked harder at the object that lay half hidden between the Dalmatian's front paws. 'Spot, what on earth have you got?'

Down went the dog's head in a guilty way. He whimpered and shuffled backwards.

'Uh-oh!' Hannah thought she recognised the chewed shape. She stooped to pick it up. 'It's Ellie's other shoe!'

'Oh, Spot!' Helen and Alexa said together.

Then all three sighed.

'More training needed, I'm afraid,' was

Alexa's verdict.

Hannah and Helen beamed and nodded.

Alexa spoke to Spot in a mock-stern voice. 'Thief catcher or not, this dog needs to learn that a baby's shoes are not for eating!'

## *Socks hitches a ride*

'David, the postman's on his way!' Mary Moore peered out of her bedroom window and spied the red van in the frosty lane. 'It looks like he could do with some help!'

'*I cad hardly mobe!*' Hannah and Helen's dad reminded her. '*By bones ache. I god da flu!*'

'Translation!' Helen lifted Socks, their young tabby cat, from the breakfast table so that Hannah could lay the plates. She went out into the narrow hall and called upstairs to her busy mum. 'Dad says he can hardly move. His bones ache. He's got the flu!'

69

'Tell him the postman's van has problems in the lane. It's skidding all over the place. Someone's got to go out and help!' Emerging from the bedroom, Mary tied her long dark hair into a ponytail, then headed to the bathroom to brush her teeth. 'Tell him I won't be able to go to work if the postman's van is blocking the lane!'

Still cuddling the soft, warm cat, Helen returned to the kitchen to relay the message.

'Uuuh!' David groaned. '*Does your mudder know I god da flu?*'

'I did tell her,' Helen assured him.

From across the farmyard they could hear the high whine of the postman's van as it struggled and skidded up the steep hill.

'*Doh symbady!*' The twins' dad shook his head and reached for his jacket on the hook behind the kitchen door.

' "No sympathy!" ' Helen translated.

Hannah looked up from her task of laying the table. Her dad's nose was red, his eyes were puffy, his skin the colour of uncooked pastry. 'Poor Dad!' she sighed. 'You stay right where you are. Helen and I will go and help the postman!'

70

'We will?' Helen imagined the icy cold air, the stiff wind blowing down from the top of the fell, the frozen puddles in the yard and on the lane.

'Yeah. C'mon, put Socks down and come with me!' Hannah flung Helen her coat. She opened the door and let in a blast of wintery air.

'*Danks*!' David sighed, sinking into a chair.

'Yeah, thanks!' Helen echoed, following Hannah outside. She noticed Socks slink through the door ahead of her and head for the barn to look for mice. 'Saturday morning, so I've got nothing better to do. Why not help push a heavy van up a mountain? I can't think of anything nicer!'

'Stop moaning!' Hannah told Helen.

The postman was clear of the patch of ice, thanks to Fred Hunt. The neighbouring farmer had spotted the problem and trundled up in his tractor, ready to tow the van.

'We didn't have to lift a finger!' Hannah said, watching the giant farm vehicle pull the red van through the gate into Home Farm.

'I'm cold!' Helen complained.

'Wimp!'

'I'm hungry!'

'Wuss!'

Fred unhitched the tow rope and backed his tractor out of the yard. He gave the twins and Bob Best, the postman, a farewell wave.

'It looks like a stack of bills and junk-mail, plus two big packages for your dad.' Bob leaned into the back of the van and lifted out the day's mail. He was a tall, thin man with a grey beard and heavy brown-rimmed glasses, wearing a regulation dark blue jacket trimmed with red. 'This one needs to be signed for.'

'Dad's got flu,' Hannah told him. 'You wouldn't want to get too close!' Taking the bulky envelopes and the postman's list of recorded delivery items, she dashed into the house.

Meanwhile, Helen went looking for Socks.

'Breakfast time!' she called as she stepped inside the dark barn across the yard from where Bob had parked his van. 'Here, Socks! Here, kitty, kitty!'

But there was only Solo in his stall. The grey pony raised his head, glad to see her after the long, cold night. He snickered and reached out over the stall door, his long white mane straggled over his eyes.

'Hello, you!' Helen went up to stroke him. She murmured a promise that she wouldn't be long. As soon as she'd fed Socks and Speckle, then had a bite to eat herself, she'd be out again to take care of him. 'It's Saturday, so it means a thorough grooming for you! And if it's not too frosty later on, Hannah and I will ride you down to Doveton Manor to meet up with Laura!'

Nudging her with his nose, Solo let her know that he approved of the plan.

'Did you see Socks?' Helen asked, looking this way and that into the dark, straw-stacked corners.

*Nudge-nudge*. Solo pleaded for more attention.

'OK, he must've snuck back to the house without me seeing.' Giving the pony a final pat, Helen headed out of the barn, just in time to see Bob Best's van inch out of the farmyard. The postman was off on his round, delivering the rest of the morning's mail to the remote farmhouses on Doveton Fell.

'Have you seen Socks?' Hannah asked Helen as she made her way back indoors. She was rattling the cat's metal food dish against the stone flags of the kitchen floor. 'Was he in the barn?'

'Nope. Isn't he in here?' Helen frowned and looked in the usual places: on the window seat, under the table, on the sofa in the front room.

'I wouldn't have asked you if he'd been in here, would I?' Hannah frowned. She went upstairs to search the bedrooms. 'Socks! Where are you?'

'Try rattling his food dish,' Mary Moore suggested, putting on her coat, ready to leave for work. 'That usually does the trick.'

'I already tried that.' Hannah's frown deepened. From the landing window she could see the red post van crawling along the lane to Crackpot Farm. 'Mum, you don't think . . . ?'

'No time to think!' Mary cut in, flying downstairs to collect her car keys. 'I'm late as usual. There'll be customers queuing up at the cafe door if I don't get a move on. See you all this evening. Have a good day. Bye!'

It was five minutes later. Their mum's car had crept steadily out of the yard and down the hill towards the village. Fred Hunt was out on the lane again, spreading salt and grit over the icy patches.

Still there was no sign of Socks's tabby face and pure white front paws creeping out from Speckle's warm basket or peering out from the airing-cupboard in the bathroom. Helen and Hannah had searched high and low.

'Helen, you don't think . . .' From the tiny bathroom window, Hannah had spied Bob Best's van snaking up the winding road towards Hardstone Pass.

Helen peered over her shoulder to see what she was looking at. 'He wouldn't . . . !' she gasped. 'Would he?'

Socks was definitely as curious as the next cat. He'd crawl into empty cardboard boxes and get stuck. There were dark roof beams in the barn which he would climb along just for the fun of it. So maybe an open door, a van full of sacks and letters, had seemed like an adventure playground to their playful cat.

Hannah's dark brown eyes grew wide. 'He would!' she gasped.

'He could've jumped in when no one was looking!' Helen cried.

'And Bob could've closed the doors without realising!' Hannah's heart sank. The red van was a tiny dot on the rugged horizon, fast disappearing into the next steep valley.

'He might jump out and get lost!' Helen groaned.

'He'll freeze to death!' Thinking the worst, Hannah raced downstairs to find their dad. 'Dad, Dad! Socks has been driven off in the post-van. What are we gonna do? He's only little, and he hasn't even had any breakfast! . . . Think of something, Dad, *please*!'

The situation was serious, David Moore agreed. '*Your mub's god da car, so we're dot bobile,*' he pointed out.

' "Mum's got the car, so we're not mobile," ' Helen translated.

'I know what he's saying; there's no need to tell me!' Worry about Socks made Hannah bad-tempered. 'He means we can't follow Bob Best and catch up with him to rescue our cat from the van!'

'What if Socks makes a run for it on High

Peak?' Helen's imagination ran riot. Once the van stopped to collect or deliver mail, one tiny tabby cat would leap out on to the frost-covered mountain. The highest fell in the area would provide no shelter. Temperatures would stay well below zero, there was nothing but rocks and windy ridges, and mile after mile of wide open space.

'Don't even think about it,' Hannah shuddered.

'*We cad delephobe da houses ob Bob's delibery route*,' their dad suggested, picking up the phone to ring the Lawsons at Crackpot Farm.

'Could we follow on foot?' Hannah wondered. 'You know; take Speckle with us and get him to track Socks down!'

'*Doh*!' David said quickly. '*Doo dangerous in dis weadder*!' He thrust the phone into Helen's hand and ordered her to explain to Sam Lawson.

For once, Sam listened to the problem and didn't mess about.

'No, sorry,' the twins' neighbour and classmate said quickly. 'Socks didn't jump out of the van when Bob called here. I went to the door to take the letters from him, so I'd have seen a tabby cat in the yard. Why not try the Cookes at Coningsby Hall? They're the next house on the postman's delivery route.'

So Helen tried Terence Cooke and his stockman, Eddie Huby, while Hannah desperately thought up other tactics to get back their beloved tabby. 'Where does Bob Best finish his round?' she asked her dad.

'*Id Desfield,*' he replied in his blocked, flu-thickened voice. '*Da sordin'-office is dear your mub's cafe, rebember?*'

Nesfield – main sorting-office – close to the Curlew Cafe. Hannah thought she knew the building he meant. It was set back from the town square, with a large yard for the delivery vans. 'Let's suppose Socks stays put in the van until Bob finishes his round . . .'

'. . . No sign of Socks at Coningsby!' Helen cut in, putting down the phone. She sounded close to tears. Visions of their little cat freezing on a wild hillside still crowded her brain. She thought back to the day she and Hannah had found him; a tiny kitten cruelly dumped in the waste-paper bin outside Luke Martin's village shop. For days they'd hand-fed him warm milk from a small dropper, until he'd gained strength and come back from the very brink of death.

'OK, like I was saying; Socks will probably have the sense to stay in the warmth all the way to Nesfield.' Hannah was determined to stay calm. 'What we should do next is phone Mum and get her to send someone round to the sorting office to wait there until Bob finishes his round.'

'Good idea!' David Moore agreed. He set up the next phone call, this time, handing the phone to Hannah.

'I understand.' Mary Moore sounded calm but concerned. 'Listen, Hannah, you and Helen will have to be patient and wait until Bob Best gets back to base here in Nesfield. I'll leave a message at the sorting-office for him to search his van and call me if he finds Socks.'

' "When"!' Hannah corrected. 'Not "if"; "when"!'

'Well, we can't be absolutely sure . . .' her mum warned. 'But in any case, there's nothing we can do except wait.'

Which Helen and Hannah felt was the hardest thing they'd ever had to do.

Wait while the clock on the kitchen wall ticked on from eight-thirty to nine.

Wait for the postman to finish delivering his letters and return to the sorting-office to unload the empty sacks and find stowaway Socks curled up asleep in the bottom of one of them . . .

'*Dry nod do build ub your hobes,*' David Moore warned the girls as they sat by the silent phone. He paced the kitchen floor, followed by a dejected Speckle.

Try not to build up your hopes! Impossible! Hannah gazed at Helen and guessed they were both thinking exactly the same thing. Because if they didn't pin all their hopes on finding Socks asleep in a letter-sack in a depot in Nesfield, they would be forced to picture him roaming the frozen fell . . .

'*Brree-brree*!'

The phone rang. Helen lunged to seize it first.

'Helen? It's me; Mum. Listen, love, I'm sorry. Bob's back and he's searched the van from top to bottom. Socks just isn't there!'

Helen felt her heart drop to the soles of her feet. Her expression told Hannah that the news was bad. Hannah sank to her knees and hugged Speckle for comfort.

So Socks was lost. He'd set out on one adventure too many, not knowing how quickly a cat could freeze to death in the wind and frost. A single night out in the open would be enough to finish him off for good.

'Search-party . . . neighbours . . . tell everyone Socks is missing!'

Hannah and Helen made plans. They couldn't just do nothing and let their poor cat die. At ten o'clock, Sam Lawson came down from Crackpot Farm with his mum, Carrie, who offered to drive the twins over Hardstone Pass, following the route which Bob Best's van had taken.

'Maybe Socks had enough sense to stick close to the road,' Sam suggested, waiting for Hannah and Helen, along with an eager Speckle, to pile into the back of their Land Rover.

Hannah allowed herself to feel a glimmer of hope. She saw Helen lean forward to grip the driver's seat, heard her urge Mrs Lawson to drive as fast as she could up the fell.

'Hold your horses,' Carrie answered, pointing out the giant yellow shape of Fred Hunt's tractor trundling down the lane towards them. 'There isn't room for two of us.'

'C'mon, Fred!' Hannah muttered, glancing round at her dad who stood in the kitchen door, muffled up in a big jumper, snuffling into a wodge of paper hankies.

The tractor rumbled and rocked, but instead of passing slowly by, it pulled up at Home Farm's gate.

'What now?' Helen murmured as she watched the old farmer climb stiffly from his cab. Perhaps Fred had come back to throw down more salt and grit on to the road. Anyway, it was no good; someone would have to point out that he was blocking their exit.

So, together she and Hannah got out of the Land Rover and ran across the yard.

'Socks is missing!' Helen began in a high, worried voice. She pointed up the fell. 'He's somewhere out there, probably freezing to death!'

'He jumped into Bob Best's post van!' Hannah explained, puzzled by the slight smile on Fred Hunt's broad face. 'He could be anywhere. We have to set out and find him before it gets dark!'

'Yes, and you two are jumping to *conclusions* as usual,' the farmer told them. 'So, before you dash off on a wild goose chase, why not come and see who I've got in my tractor cab?'

'Who?' Helen narrowed her eyes and glanced at the machine, then at Hannah.

'Guess!'

'Who?' Hannah insisted, breaking into a run, through the gate and out into the lane.

Please, please let it be who she suspected! Let it be a small, striped, black and brown furry creature with a black tail, long whiskers and two sparkling white front paws.

'Socks!' Helen climbed on the huge black tractor tyre and peered into the cab.

There he lay, curled up behind the seat; the place which he'd chosen when Fred had first brought out the tractor to tow Bob Best's van up the frozen hill. The farmer told them that the little cat had snoozed undiscovered until just now, when his wife, Hilda, had spotted him.

'Socks!' Hannah scolded, reaching into the cab.

Socks opened one yellow eye, then the other. He blinked and yawned, showing them his long, rough tongue and the ridged arch of the roof of his mouth. What's the fuss? he seemed to say. Can't a cat take a nap when he feels like it?

Hannah took him in both hands and drew him to her. He purred and cuddled close.

'Don't ever give us a fright like that again!' Helen sighed as everyone gathered round.

'*Doh, don't*!' David Moore agreed.

*Who, me*? Stripey Socks snuggled against Hannah, took one look at the windswept clouds, the frost-covered walls and hedges of the remote hillside, then promptly went straight back to sleep.

## *Samson in trouble*

'Come here, my angel!' Pauline Merton, the retired postmistress of Nesfield post office, tempted Sybil with half a custard-cream.

The silky-haired little Yorkshire terrier hurled herself across the garden to snatch the treat.

'You see; she's so obedient!' Miss Merton smiled fondly at her pint-sized pet.

*Crunch-crunch-gobble*. The dog devoured the biscuit.

'She does absolutely everything she's told!' the old lady cooed. 'She sits when I ask her. She walks to heel. She stops at the kerb whenever we want to cross the road.'

'Very good,' David Moore mumbled, unconvinced, his own mouth full of jammy dodger. He, Helen and Hannah had been invited to tea at Miss Merton's house so that she could discuss a portrait sitting for Sybil. The twins' dad had told the neat, grey-haired lady what he would charge for a giant, full-colour photo of the pampered Yorkie.

'Who's a good little doggy?' With a soppy voice and look, Miss Merton held up another piece of biscuit. 'See, she begs so nicely!'

'She'd better watch out. Sybil could bite her hand off if she goes on like that!' Hannah mumbled to Helen.

A long, grey and fawn fringe covered the terrier's brown eyes, but you could still see the gleam there. The gleam said, 'FOOD!' in big letters. A micro-second later, the litle dog had jumped and snatched.

'Oh, Sybil!' Miss Merton withdrew her hand just in time. Then quickly she smoothed things over. 'Of course, she didn't mean anything by that. She's just a little poppet, a complete charmer, aren't you, darling?'

*Gobble-gobble-gulp*. The biscuit was gone.

'And, as I was telling my brother, Peter, she's good company for me since I retired from my job . . .'

*Scrabble-scrabble-scratch*. Sybil jumped up at her mistress's knee, demanding more treats. Her pink tongue licked Miss Merton's skinny hand; her sharp, pointed teeth tugged at the hem of the grey, pleated skirt.

'So when would you like me to take Sybil's photo?' David finished his cup of tea and stood up from the low deckchair. He signalled to the girls that it was time to go.

Helen and Hannah didn't need telling twice. They loved all animals, but Miss Merton was beginning to get on their nerves with her 'angels', 'darlings' and 'poppets'.

In any case, they'd seen Karl Thomas's van arrive outside his house further along Rose Terrace, and watched over the garden wall now as he bundled Samson, the giant Old English sheepdog, out of the back.

'Hi, Karl!' Helen called to their painter and decorator friend.

'Hi, Samson!' Hannah grinned as the enormous, shaggy grey and white dog loped along the pavement to see them.

'*Woof*!' Samson roared, rearing up and resting his huge forepaws on Miss Merton's wall. His friendly growl sounded like a motor bike engine revving up.

'Oh look, Sybil!' Pauline Merton scooped her miniature terrier into her arms and brought him to say hello. 'It's your friend, Samson!'

'*Yip*!' Sybil squirmed with delight and wagged her tail at the visitor.

'You mean the two of them get on?' Helen turned to Miss Merton in surprise. Sybil and Samson would be an unlikely pairing; the Little and Large of the dog world.

'Like a house on fire,' Karl assured her as he strode up in his paint-spattered overalls. 'Listen, it's my lunchtime. I don't suppose you and Hannah would fancy . . . ?'

'Taking Samson for a walk! You bet!' Helen jumped in. She shot through the gate to take Samson's lead. 'We'll go down by the lake. What time do you want him back?'

'*Yip-yip. yip-yip*!' As the arrangements were made, Sybil wriggled free from Miss Merton's thin arms and squeezed through the gate on to the pavement. She bounced up against Samson, who sat steady as a rock with a bemused look on his hairy face.

'She wants to go too!' Miss Merton interpreted. She looked expectantly at Hannah. 'Erm . . . er . . . would it be all right?'

Hannah swallowed hard. 'Of course!'

The ex-postmistress beamed and hurried inside. 'Then wait here a moment while I get Sybil's lead!'

'Well!' Hannah sighed.

It wasn't so much a case of Helen and her taking Samson and Sybil for a walk as the other way around.

The giant and the midget pulled them along, tugging them around lamp-posts and across Nesfield's main square, past the Curlew cafe.

'Well, what?' Helen demanded. Her arm was practically wrenched out of its socket by the big dog's eagerness to be down at the lakeside.

'Well, I could hardly say no!' Hannah insisted.

Helen had been giving her black looks all the way from Rose Terrace. 'And it's not Sybil's fault that she's a little brat. Miss Merton is spoiling her!' It was the same old story; bad owner equals naughty dog.

'*Yip-yap-yip*!' Sybil barked and snarled at a passing cyclist. She was a small ball of fury, teeth bared, jaws snapping.

' "Little angel . . . little poppet"!' Helen mimicked the terrier's owner. 'She sets Samson off too. Look, he doesn't usually pull at the lead like this!'

The sheepdog strained to keep up with Sybil and tugged Helen down a narrow alleyway that led to the lake.

'*Yii-iip*!' Sybil spotted a black cat on a low slate roof. She leaped straight into the air as if she was on springs.

Slowly the cat stood and arched his back. He hissed down at the passing group, then just as lazily settled back into his sunny spot.

'Phew!' Crossing the final road, Helen was relieved to let Samson off the lead. He shook himself, then put his nose to the ground, following interesting scents across the pebbly beach.

Hannah too was glad to let Sybil have a free run. That was, until the Yorkshire terrier pricked up her ears and got the old glint in her eye. 'Uh-oh! She's spotted that group having a picnic by the water . . . Sybil, come back! Sybil, no!'

No good. The mini-dog set off like a whirlwind across the pebbles. Samson meanwhile lumbered on, sniffing nice scents and minding his own business.

*Whoosh*! The silver and fawn tornado smelled biscuit. Children wailed and scattered to right and left. Mothers shouted 'Shoo!' and waved their arms. Sybil gobbled as fast as she could.

'Sorry! Excuse me . . . sorry . . . oh dear!' Hannah stumbled after the picnic wrecker, too late to stop Sybil from devouring two Kit-Kats and a Jaffa cake.

Meanwhile, Samson plodded on by the water's edge. He picked up a branch of driftwood and dragged it towards Helen, good temperedly asking her to throw it for him to fetch. 'It's too big to lift!' she told him. 'And Sybil's just landed us in a whole heap of trouble. We'd better move on as fast as we can, as soon as Hannah's finished

offering to pay for the biscuits that pesky little
dog just scoffed!'

' "Come here, my angel!" ' Hannah muttered under
her breath.

Sybil had avoided capture amongst the
wreckage of the picnic and hared off across the
beach towards a wooden jetty. Samson was still
blithely dragging half a tree along the water's edge.
Little and Large. Laurel and Hardy. If you thought
about it, it was a funny sight.

' "Angel"!' Hannah frowned and gazed at Sybil
through narrowed eyes.

'If looks could kill, that little dog would be well
and truly zapped!' Helen laughed.

'Well!' Hannah felt hot and red. The picnicking
mothers had given her a hard time.

' "Bad owner equals naughty dog," remember!'

Hannah wasn't in the mood. 'Well!' she
muttered darkly, unable to put into words what
she felt about Miss Merton's precious pooch. 'I
mean, look at Samson. He's six times Sybil's size
and he hasn't given us a scrap of trouble!'

'No, but I wish he'd drop that tree trunk!'

For a few seconds, Helen and Hannah turned their back on Sybil to encourage Samson to put down the branch. He barked happily and bounded towards them, his hairy feet wet from scampering along the lake shore.

And those few seconds were long enough for Sybil to get up to her neck in trouble once more.

She reached the jetty and spied another family.

'Oh no!' Hannah looked round.

'*Waaa-aaack*!' This time, the mother was small, speckled and feathered. The children waddled and ran ahead of the charging terrier. '*Wak-wak-wak*!' the mother duck cried.

'Sybil, come back!' Helen yelled, setting off along the jetty. She pictured feathers flying, a tragic end to one small duckling's day.

To the twins' surprise, Samson decided to help. He lolloped on to the jetty to bring Sybil back and began to pound along the wooden boards. A middle-aged man in a nearby rowing boat looked up, then cried out in alarm at the awesome sight.

'Ohhhh!' Hannah closed her eyes, unable to look.

*Plop*! One young duck swerved sideways and

dived to safety. *Plop-plop-plop*! Three more jumped over the edge of the jetty, disappeared below the surface, then bobbed back into view.

'*Waaa-aaack*!' the mother duck yelled at Sybil and Samson as they galloped by.

At the far end of the jetty, little Sybil braked and stopped. Clumsy Samson missed his footing and lumbered on. And on.

'Eeek!' Helen made a squealing noise.

Samson reached the end. His front paws met not boards but thin air. They scrabbled madly as he fought to control his rear end. Then he took a nose dive.

*Neeyah . . . splash*!

Over forty kilos of Old English sheepdog hit the water.

'What the . . . !' The man in the boat swore, threw down his oars and clung to the sides.

'*Wak-wak-wak*!' The mother duck hurried her brood away from the spreading tidal wave.

'Samson!' Hannah and Helen squawked.

Waves lapped the jetty, sprayed up and soaked them through. Then the giant dog broke the surface, fur flattened and streaming, black nose

like a giant button on a squashed white face.

'Keep that dog under control, why don't you!' the oarsman yelled as Samson swam for the shore.

'It wasn't Sam . . .' Helen began.

'It was Syb . . .' Hannah tried to explain.

'Oh, never mind!' they said together, making a run for it, hard on the heels of the nippy little terrier. 'Sorry!' they sang out, hoping never to see the angry man again.

'Come on, Samson, you can do it!' Hannah urged. She jumped from the jetty on to the shore and watched him make slow progress.

'*Yip-yip-yip*!' Sybil careered off along the pebbles, looking for more picnics.

At last, the big dog reached dry land.

'Thank heavens!' Helen breathed. 'At least we didn't have to jump in and rescue him!'

'No, we stayed dry . . .' Hannah agreed, dashing forward to make sure that Samson was OK.

He plodded out of the water, stopped, then shook himself from head to toe. Water sprayed everywhere. Droplets rose and sparkled in the sun's rays. They spattered down over Hannah and Helen, on to the jetty, into the boat where the furious man crouched.

'I'm soaked!' he yelled, standing up, losing his balance, waving his arms as the boat rocked. 'Wo-o-oah!'

And he tipped and landed in the water, spluttering and splashing.

Helen glanced at Hannah. 'What now?'

Hannah grabbed Samson's collar and looked round wildly for Sybil, the cause of all this bother. The Yorkshire terrier appeared from behind a big rock, licking her mysteriously chocolate-covered lips . . . Hannah didn't even want to think about it!

'Run!' Helen suggested.

And the four of them – Sybil, Samson, Hannah and Helen – left the beach!

'It wasn't Samson's fault!' Helen tried to explain to Karl Thompson how come his giant dog was soaked to the skin. 'It was Syb . . .'

'Oh, thank heavens you didn't drown, my poor angel!' Miss Merton gathered her beloved pet to her.

David Moore stood by, camera in hand, giving

the twins a curious look.

Their short dark hair was windswept, their faces were red, they were gasping and breathless after their rapid retreat from the lake.

'Sybil ate someone's picnic!' Hannah muttered out of the corner of her mouth.

She might as well have saved her breath. 'Did Samson get you into trouble, my poor poppet?' Miss Merton cried. 'He's a big, big dog, remember. Little dogs like you must stay out of his way!'

Helen noticed the corners of her dad's mouth begin to twitch.

'Erm, if you don't mind, I think it's time we settled down to take Sybil's picture.' He told Miss Merton that there was no time like the present, so the old lady began to fuss with comb and brush.

'Now, sit, petal! Let Mummy make you look nice and pretty for your photograph!'

'Samson was only trying to stop the little pest getting into more trouble!' Helen whispered to Karl. 'Really, he's completely innocent!'

Still bedraggled, the big dog hung his head.

Miss Merton preened Sybil and arranged her on a red, yellow and black checked blanket. The little dog's coat shone like silver silk; she wore a topnotch tied with red ribbon on her head.

'Ready?' David Moore asked.

Miss Merton nodded then stepped back.

'. . . We could go and find witnesses for you!' Hannah assured Samson's owner. 'Loads of people saw Sybil being naughty and Samson being good!'

'. . . Ah, Peter!' The retired postmistress heard the click of the garden gate and turned to greet her brother. 'Oh my goodness!' she gasped in sudden shock.

*Squelch-squelch-squelch*! A figure walked up the path, shoes oozing water, clothes dripping wet.

The man in the boat was Miss Merton's brother!

Helen's mouth fell open. Hannah stepped forward to hide Samson from view.

Peter Merton spied the big, shaggy dog nonetheless.

'Better get Samson out of here!' Hannah hissed at Karl.

'But I thought you said it was Syb . . . !' The painter couldn't keep up. He was confused.

'It was. But Mr Merton thinks it was Samson . . .

just go!' Helen had to accept that sometimes life simply wasn't fair.

So Karl and Samson beat another hasty retreat.

And, as he went into the house, Peter Merton grumbled about giant dogs being out of control.

And Pauline Merton said how glad she was that she only had a miniature poppet like Sybil to look after.

David Moore pointed his camera at one beautiful Yorkie, who peered back at him through a blonde fringe of silken hair.

'A big dog like Samson would be such a handful!' Miss Merton tutted. 'Now, smile, Sybil, there's a little darling!'

*Click-click*. The twins' dad got the perfect portrait.

Helen and Hannah secretly fumed. *Poser! Fake*!

There was a glint in the little dog's eye. *Prove it*!

*One day*! Hannah and Helen swore. *Your luck will run out, Sybil; just you wait*!

# *Poor Solo*

'Dad, can you NOT sing, please!' Helen sat in the back of the car, hands over her ears.

'Yeah, Dad; you sound like a cow in pain!' Hannah giggled.

David Moore ignored them both.

' "*Summertime . . . and the livin' is easy, Fish are jumpin', and the cotton is high*!" '

The twins' mum glanced over her shoulder with a raised eyebrow. 'You're just encouraging him!' she warned.

'Moo-ooo!' Helen groaned tunelessly.

' "*Daddy's rich . . . and your momma's*

*good-lookin'* ".'

'Hah!' Hannah yelped.

'And that's enough of *that*, young lady!' Mary said primly.

Then they all burst out laughing so hard that David almost steered into the grass verge at the side of the lane.

'Lucky I'm not the sensitive type,' he said with a broad grin as he drove through the gates of Home Farm. 'It could make me feel very down, the amount of criticism I get from you lot!'

'Water off a duck's back!' The first out of the car, Mary went to unlock the door.

Speckle came bounding out of the house to greet them after their trip to the supermarket. He made a bee-line for Hannah and Helen, wagging his tail and making eager whining noises.

Helen stroked him. 'Hey, anyone would think we'd been gone ages!'

Speckle barked and ran a few steps across the yard. He barked again, came back to the girls, then repeated the sequence.

'He wants us to follow him.' Hannah recognised the signal. 'Look, he's heading for the field.'

'What about the shopping?' Their dad was already struggling into the house with the first box of groceries.

Speckle barked again, more urgently this time.

'We won't be long,' Helen promised. It was unlike the dog to be so impatient. 'We'll just see what Speckle wants!'

So she and Hannah ran after him, round the side of the house and over the low stone wall into the field where they kept their pony.

The grass sloped upwards towards the wild fell; a breeze blew through the trees and fluttered their leaves.

'Where's Solo?' At first Helen couldn't see the familiar figure; not until Speckle barked again and raced around the back of the horse chestnut tree which gave the pony shade and shelter. Following him, both she and Hannah found out why the field had felt so empty and strange.

Solo was down on his side, his head in the dirt. His legs were bent under him, his dappled grey sides heaving, and when he saw the twins he gave a pitiful, weak snicker.

'Oh, poor Solo!' Hannah dropped to her knees

beside him. 'Oh, Helen, he's hurt! What are we going to do?'

'Don't try to get him to move. Wait here. I'll fetch help!' In a flash Helen took in what had happened. Solo must have had some kind of accident and whinnied as he'd gone down. Speckle had heard the cry of pain from inside the house. That was why he'd been so anxious to bring them out here. 'Good dog!' she murmured as he lay down close to Solo's head. Then she turned and ran.

'Solo, Solo!' Hannah cried. She stayed with him, stroking his neck, but almost afraid to touch him. She'd never seen him like this; helpless and in pain. His eyes were half closed; his head seemed too heavy to lift from the trampled patch of earth. 'It's going to be OK!' she promised. 'Helen will fetch the vet. We're going to make you better!'

'What's the verdict?' Mary Moore asked Sally Freeman.

The worried group had gathered in the field around the injured pony. They'd helped the vet to raise Solo to his feet and watched as she examined him. Now Sally was putting away her stethoscope and closing up her first-aid kit.

'Hmm.' She half-frowned, half-smiled.

Hannah and Helen hung on every gesture, every flicker of expression. How serious was it?

Solo was wobbly on his feet, his white mane tangled with twigs and grass. His head hung low and he still looked dazed and confused.

'Well?' David prompted.

'He's damaged the tendon in one of his front legs,' Sally explained. 'He probably stumbled and went down heavily on it. It wouldn't take much; horses' legs are very susceptible to this kind of injury.'

Hannah held her breath as she listened. She had pictures in her head of the old days, when they shot a horse who'd gone lame.

'You see this swelling around the knee joint? That's where the problem is; where the tendon is attached to the bone.' The vet bent to show them. 'We can put a cold compress on the joint to ease the swelling, but the process of healing is a long one, I'm afraid.'

Helen stood close to Solo, stroking and soothing

him. She could feel him tremble as Sally touched the injured knee, saw that his coat was hot and sweaty in patches after the painful struggle to raise him to his feet.

'How long?' Mary, the practical one, asked the important question.

'Six weeks. Which means, we have to get him in from the field and put him in the stable for that length of time. We call it box-rest; no exercise, a complete lay-off.'

Breathing again, Hannah got over the shock. 'And after six weeks he'll be OK?'

Sally nodded and her face relaxed. 'Oh yes, don't worry. This isn't a matter of life and death. If he gets the right treatment, Solo will be fine!'

'But poor Solo!' Hannah sighed. 'It must have been horrible for him to fall over and find that he couldn't get up again!'

'With nobody around to help,' Helen agreed.

Sally Freeman had bandaged the injured knee and left the pony in his stable still looking sorry for himself. 'It's very important that you don't work him until the six weeks is up,' she'd insisted.

'I know that means he's out of action for the whole of your summer holiday, but I'm afraid that's the way it has to be!'

And they'd promised faithfully that they'd keep Solo safe inside his stall, well fed and comfortable, but definitely not allowing him back out into the field, however much he begged them to let him get at the juicy green grass.

'And definitely no riding him!' Sally had stressed. 'Sorry!'

Helen and Hannah had agreed once more and kept their chins up until the grown-ups had retreated into the house for a cup of tea.

But, 'No riding!' Helen sighed as soon as they were alone with the pony.

Hannah shook her head. 'I suppose it's not that bad. We've got our bikes.'

'Bikes!' Helen grunted. 'Not the same, is it?'

'No. But it's worse for Solo.' Hannah tried to be big about it, but she admitted it was hard to be deprived of those brilliant rides out on to the fell: the wind tugging at your sweatshirt, Solo's tail swishing away the flies, the creak of the leather saddle, the clink of the metal bit and bridle . . .

\* \* \*

'We're making good progress!'

It was two weeks after Solo's fall and Sally Freeman was prepared to relent.

'He's really fed up!' Hannah told the vet as they stood inside the barn, discussing their next move.

'He's bored!' Helen insisted.

'And getting fat!' Hannah patted Solo's round belly. 'All this food and no exercise.'

'You've done well with the box-rest,' Sally told them, trying not to smile. 'I must say, you've been very patient. And it must have been hard, watching all your friends riding up the lane past the house, without being able to join in.'

'Yeah!' the twins sighed. Laura Saunders came by every day on Sultan, and sometimes she was with Polly Moone on Holly. Hannah and Helen had stood at the gate sadly watching.

'So can we let him out?' Hannah asked.

Sally nodded. 'He can come out of his stall into the field, as long as you can fence him inside a small square with electric tape.' She described how they must stake out an area of grass, then link up the stakes with a metallic ribbon which would give Solo a slight electric shock whenever he touched it. 'He'll soon learn to stay inside the fence. That way, he'll be out in the fresh air, eating grass, without any danger of him using the injured leg too much.'

Everyone agreed it was a good plan.

'Except that we don't have any of the special fencing,' the twins' dad pointed out, when they went to explain. 'And I expect it's pretty expensive . . .'

'I'll bet Laura's got some!' Helen came up with a solution. 'We could go down to the manor and borrow hers!'

Everyone nodded. 'Slow but sure,' Mrs Freeman recommended. 'And remember, even though Solo's knee looks a lot better, there's still no slapping a saddle on to his back and taking him out for a ride!'

'Not even a teeny little one?' Hannah pleaded.

'Not even around the field!' Sally insisted. It was her final word. She climbed into her Land Rover and left Helen and Hannah standing with Solo cooped up inside his tiny, old, cobwebby stall.

\* \* \*

'Sure you can borrow the fencing!' Laura told them brightly. She and Polly had just returned from their morning ride, and the two girls were unsaddling Sultan and walking him out into the paddock when Helen and Hannah arrived.

'We don't want it for nothing!' Helen assured her. 'We'll do something for you to keep things equal.'

Hannah knew why Helen had said this. The Saunderses were much richer than the Moores; they had rows of shining tack in the tack-room, an immaculate stable yard. Helen's offer was intended to keep a kind of balance between them. 'We could do some work for you,' she volunteered as they followed Laura and Polly into the lush green field.

Laura unbuckled Sultan's headcollar and let him wander off to join Scott and Heather, the two piebald Shetland ponies. 'Hey, that would be great!' she agreed. 'And it just so happens, Mum wants me to go with her to see an aunt in London this coming Saturday. Which means I won't be around to look after the horses. I was going to ask you if you'd mind coming down . . .'

'Brilliant!' Helen and Hannah chimed in.

'Saturday!' Hannah promised, as they collected the stakes and metallic tape from a store room in the yard.

Helen was eager to get back home. 'Don't worry, leave Sultan, Scott and Heather to us. They'll be absolutely fine!'

' "*Summertime*!" ' Helen sang in a low, low voice. She shovelled up soiled straw from Sultan's stable and pitched it into a wheelbarrow. ' "*And the livin' is eas-y*!" '

'Not you too!' Hannah protested. She got enough of that from her dad at home.

Helen wheeled the barrow off across the yard. 'Sorry!'

' "*. . . Fish are jumpin' and the cotton is high*," ' Hannah hummed. 'Oops!'

There was new straw to lay, Sultan to be brushed and turned out into the paddock . . . a hundred and one things to do before Laura returned.

And back at Home Farm, Solo was nibbling grass inside his special little area. The stakes were staked, the tapes taped.

'Doesn't he look chuffed!' the twins' mum had said, on her way out to the car.

'It's as if he got out of prison!' their dad had pointed out. 'He's been banged up in the jug, and now he's free!'

Solo had looked up and whinnied his thanks. He'd limped slowly across to show them that the leg was improving, then he'd gone and got on with the serious business of eating.

They'd come down to Doveton Manor to fulfil their promise and at the same time do one of their favourite things of looking after horses.

'If you can't ride 'em, muck 'em out!' Helen quipped, whistling as she worked. She got out a couple of brushes, tossed one to Hannah, then began to brush Sultan's rich brown coat. 'Easy, boy!' ' she murmured when he stamped his foot and snorted.

'He heard a car pulling up.' Curious, Hannah looked out over the stable door. 'It's the Moones,' she whispered, recognising the slight, sandy-haired woman from the riding stables at nearby Manor Farm and her plumper, dark-haired daughter. 'I wonder what they want!'

Helen worked steadily while Hannah dealt with the visitors. 'Good boy!' she murmured, gently brushing around the tall thoroughbred's ears. He blew through his nostrils and turned to nudge her hand, enjoying the pampering and Helen's soft touch.

'Hi, Hannah!' Polly said brightly. Her long hair was tied back, she wore jodhpurs and a red T-shirt. 'I told Mum that this was where you'd be!'

'You came specially to see us?' This puzzled Hannah more than ever. After all, she and Helen hardly knew the Moones, who were new to Doveton. They'd moved into Manor Farm, done it up, started a riding school, were making a success of it. But why would Polly's mum seek them out?

Linda Moone nodded. 'You're making a nice job of Sultan,' she told Helen.

Helen blushed. 'Thanks.'

'And the stable looks spick and span.' Mrs Moone cast an approving eye over the place.

Hannah frowned at Polly. 'What's up?' she whispered.

'Nothing.' Polly grinned. 'Mum, don't keep them in suspense. Explain!'

Mrs Moone leaned casually on the door. 'Well, the truth is, I'm a bit short of help at Manor Farm right now,' she told them. 'A couple of members of staff have gone on holiday, so I could do with someone to muck out stables and so on.'

Helen stopped brushing Sultan and stepped forward to join Hannah.

'Interested?' Linda Moone smiled.

'Yeah!' they nodded. More work with horses! They knew the Moones kept Shetlands and Welsh ponies, two or three Arabs and some gorgeous ex-racehorses. 'You bet!'

'It wouldn't be a proper job; just a kind of casual arrangement. You're both too young for me to pay you a wage or anything . . .'

'We don't care!' Helen assured her. Like she'd just said to Hannah, 'If you can't ride 'em, muck 'em out!'

'No, it doesn't matter!' Hannah echoed. 'We like being round horses; honest!'

'That's what Polly told me.' Linda Moone seemed half impressed, half amused. 'She also said you love to ride?'

'Yes, but . . .' Hannah began.

'. . . We can't at the moment. Solo's hurt his leg,' Helen finished.

Mrs Moone nodded. 'So what do you say to riding the ponies at Manor Farm in return for the work you put in?'

Hannah gasped and looked at Helen.

Helen's eyes shone.

What did they say? 'Oh, wow! Cool! Excellent!'

'So you see, Solo, it's not that we don't care about you!' Helen explained.

'No, so there's no need to be jealous!' Hannah was worried that their faithful grey pony would sulk when he saw them ride up the lane for the first time on two of the riding school horses. Helen was on a black Welsh pony called Horace, she was on a chestnut Connemara called Kelly. Behind them came Laura on Sultan and Polly Moone on Holly.

Solo had poked his head over the wall at the clip-clop of hooves. Speckle too had come running out of the farmyard.

'Don't feel bad,' Helen went on, dismounting and leading the sturdy Welsh pony towards Solo.

'We're helping Mrs Moone to exercise her horses. Believe us, this is work!'

Solo stared hard at Helen in her riding-hat and her fat, short-legged mount.

'We still love you best!' Hannah told him earnestly. 'Honest!'

Their injured pony turned his head to give Kelly the once-over. He dismissed the chestnut with a toss of his mane. Then he strolled off with hardly a limp to watch Speckle bound down the length of the field, through buttercups and daisies.

'He couldn't care less!' David Moore had come out from the house. 'If you ask me, he's planning to make the most of his six weeks holiday!'

'You're sure he's OK?' Hannah said anxiously.

'Fine!' her dad insisted. 'No need for you two to look so guilty!'

'He doesn't feel left out?' Helen queried.

'Does he seem upset?' David shook his head and laughed.

Hannah and Helen gazed at Solo. He'd gone down on to his side and rolled lazily, legs in the air. Then he eased himself upright, shook himself and ambled away.

'Well on the mend, wouldn't you say?' the twins' dad teased.

Slowly they nodded.

'So!' David offered Helen a leg up on to Horace.

'So?' Hannah was torn. If she was honest, half of her *wanted* Solo to mind. She almost wished that he was there at the wall, barging and bossing, demanding to come with them.

But he wasn't. He was too busy playing with Speckle.

'So, go!' their dad ordered. 'Solo will still be here when you get back. There'll be hundreds more times when you're saddling the poor guy and dragging him on to the fell, believe me!'

He was right, of course.

And Home Farm would be here, with Speckle and Socks, the ducks, the geese, the rabbits . . .

Hannah waited until Helen was ready, then turned to face up the hill.

' "*Summertime* . . ." ' their dad hummed. ' ". . . *and the livin' is easy*!" '

Solo whinnied. Speckle barked. With happy sighs, the twins rode ahead of Laura and Polly, on up the lane.

# HOME FARM TWINS
## *Jenny Oldfield*

| | | | |
|---|---|---|---|
| 66127 5 | Speckle The Stray | £3.99 | ❏ |
| 66128 3 | Sinbad The Runaway | £3.99 | ❏ |
| 66129 1 | Solo The Homeless | £3.99 | ❏ |
| 66130 5 | Susie The Orphan | £3.99 | ❏ |
| 66131 3 | Spike The Tramp | £3.99 | ❏ |
| 66132 1 | Snip and Snap The Truants | £3.99 | ❏ |
| 68990 0 | Sunny The Hero | £3.99 | ❏ |
| 68991 9 | Socks The Survivor | £3.99 | ❏ |
| 68992 7 | Stevie The Rebel | £3.99 | ❏ |
| 68993 5 | Samson The Giant | £3.99 | ❏ |
| 69983 3 | Sultan The Patient | £3.99 | ❏ |
| 69984 1 | Sorrel The Substitute | £3.99 | ❏ |
| 69985 X | Skye The Champion | £3.99 | ❏ |
| 69986 8 | Sugar and Spice The Pickpockets | £3.99 | ❏ |
| 69987 6 | Sophie The Show-off | £3.99 | ❏ |
| 72682 2 | Smoky The Mystery | £3.99 | ❏ |
| 72795 0 | Scott The Braveheart | £3.99 | ❏ |
| 72796 9 | Spot The Prisoner | £3.99 | ❏ |
| 727977 | Shelley The Shadow | £3.99 | ❏ |

*All Hodder Children's books are available at your local bookshop, or can be ordered direct from the publisher. Just tick the titles you would like and complete the details below. Prices and availability are subject to change without prior notice.*

Please enclose a cheque or postal order made payable to *Bookpoint Ltd*, and send to: Hodder Children's Books, 39 Milton Park, Abingdon, OXON OX14 4TD, UK. Email Address: orders@bookpoint.co.uk

If you would prefer to pay by credit card, our call centre team would be delighted to take your order by telephone. Our direct line *01235 400414* (lines open 9.00 am–6.00 pm Monday to Saturday, 24 hour message answering service). Alternatively you can send a fax on *01235 400454*.

| TITLE | | FIRST NAME | | SURNAME | |
|---|---|---|---|---|---|

| ADDRESS | |
|---|---|
| | |
| | |
| | |

| DAYTIME TEL: | | POST CODE | |
|---|---|---|---|

If you would prefer to pay by credit card, please complete:
Please debit my Visa/Access/Diner's Card/American Express (delete as applicable) card no:

| | | | | | | | | | | | | | | | | | |
|---|---|---|---|---|---|---|---|---|---|---|---|---|---|---|---|---|---|

Signature ........................................................ Expiry Date: ................................

If you would NOT like to receive further information on our products please tick the box. ❐